caillou®

Walks His Dog

Adaptation of the original text by Roger Harvey, based on the animated series
Illustrations taken from the television series

 chouette   COOKIE JAR

Caillou was playing catch with Daddy.
"Throw me the ball," Caillou said.
The ball slipped between Caillou's legs
and rolled out onto the sidewalk.
Woof woof!
Grandma appeared with a little white
dog on a leash.
"Hello, Caillou," Grandma said.

"Hey, it's Alfred!" Caillou said. He bent down to pet it. The dog licked Caillou's face, and Caillou laughed.
"I'm looking after Alfred today," Grandma said. "Would you like to walk the dog with me, Caillou?"

"Can I hold the leash?" Caillou
asked Grandma.
"Of course," she said.
Beaming proudly, Caillou held the
leash with both hands and set off
to walk Alfred.
When they reached the corner
of their street, the dog stopped and
promptly sat down.

"He's waiting for you to tell him it's okay to cross the street. Say 'walk' when it's safe," Grandma explained.
Caillou looked left and right and saw that the road was clear.
"Walk," he said.
Alfred got up and trotted across the street. Caillou was delighted that the dog obeyed his command.

At the park, Grandma took a ball from her pocket. "Look what I brought you, Alfred." When he saw the ball, Alfred started barking excitedly.
Woof woof!

"Throw the ball for him, Caillou, and say, 'fetch'!"
The dog was watching Caillou intently and wagging his tail.
Caillou threw the ball as far as he could.
"Fetch!" he said.

The dog raced after the ball and brought it right back.
"He did it!" Caillou shouted.
Alfred had the ball in his mouth and was waiting for another command.
"Tell him, 'drop it'," Grandma said.
Obediently, Alfred dropped the ball.

Caillou made up more games.
He dug a hole in the sand and
buried the ball. Alfred started to dig
furiously, throwing up sand in all
directions.
Triumphantly, he brought the ball
back to Caillou. Caillou was thrilled
and hugged the dog.

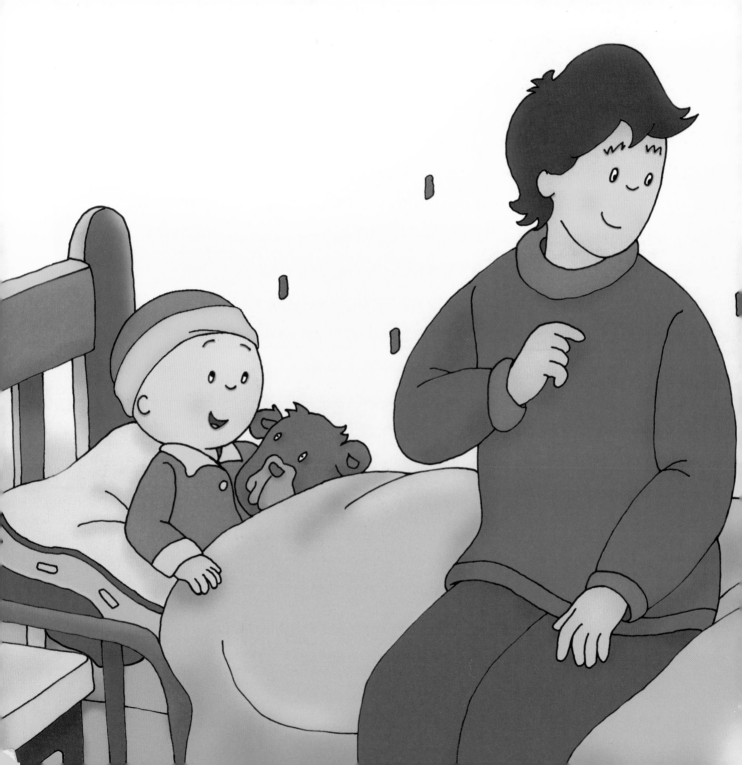

That night when Daddy came in to tuck him in, Caillou said,"Daddy, I'd really, really like a little white dog."
"I know Alfred's very cute, but we already have a pet. We have Gilbert." Daddy said.
When he heard his name, the cat opened one eye.

"But I want a dog, a dog I can take for walks," Caillou insisted. "When you and Rosie are a little older, we'll talk about it again, okay?" Daddy said, tucking Caillou in. "Good night, Caillou."

The next morning, Caillou rummaged through his toy box and pulled out a stuffed toy dog and a piece of string. "Here's a leash for you," he said and tied the string around the dog's neck. Caillou went downstairs, "Mommy, Daddy, I've got a surprise!"

"What is it?" Daddy asked sleepily.
"I've got a surprise. Look!" Caillou laughed and started
to run around the room with the dog on the leash.

"Caillou, doggy!"
Rosie exclaimed.
Caillou picked up the
stuffed dog and
rubbed his face gently
in its soft fur.
Now Caillou had his
very own dog he
could walk every day.

Text adapted by Roger Harvey based on the scenario of the CAILLOU animated film series produced by Cookie Jar Entertainment Inc. (© 1997 CINAR Productions (2004) Inc., a subsidiary of Cookie Jar Entertainment Inc.).
All rights reserved.

Original story written by Christel Kleitch.
Illustrations taken from the television series CAILLOU.
Graphic design: Monique Dupras
Computer graphics: Les Studios de la Souris Mécanique

The PBS KIDS logo is a registered mark of PBS and is used with permission.

We acknowledge the financial support of the Government of Canada through the Canada Book Fund for our publishing activities.

Canadian Heritage   Patrimoine canadien

We acknowledge the support of the Ministry of Culture and Communications of Quebec and SODEC for the publication and promotion of this book.

SODEC
Québec

Bibliothèque et Archives nationales du Québec and Library and Archives Canada cataloguing in publication

Harvey, Roger, 1940-
Caillou walks his dog
New ed.
(Clubhouse)
Translation of: Caillou promène son chien.
For children aged 3 and up.

ISBN 978-2-89450-814-5

1. Dogs -Juvenile literature. 2. Children and animals - Juvenile literature. I. Title.
II. Series: Clubhouse.

SF426.5.H3613 2011 j636.7   C2010-942033-0

Legal deposit: 2011

Printed in China
10 9 8 7 6 5 4 3 2 CHO1891 JUL2013